GOODIES AND BADDIES

Compiled by Pat Edwards and Wendy Body

Acknowledgements

We are grateful to the following for permission to reproduce copyright material: Hamish Hamilton Ltd for the story 'Wildcat Wendy and The Peekaboo Kid' by Nancy Chambers; Penguin Books Ltd for the poem 'Nothing, that's what' from p.38 *Wry Rhymes For Troublesome Times* by Max Fatchen (Kestrel Books, 1983) Copyright © Max Fatchen 1983; Spike Milligan Productions Ltd for the poem 'Updated Hubbard' from *Unspun Socks From a Chicken's Laundry* by Spike Milligan; The Bodley Head and Greenwillow Books (A Division of William Morrow & Co.) for extracts from the short stories 'Mr and Mrs Ramsbottom', 'The Robbers' and 'The Tractor Chase' from pp.32-53 *Follow that Bus* by Pat Hutchins Copyright © 1977 by Pat Hutchins. Contributors for pages 50-53: Bill Boyle and Sarah Shaps.

We have been unable to trace the copyright holder in the story 'Sherluck Bones at The Biscuit Factory' from *The Sherluck Bones Mystery Detective Book* by Jim & Mary Razz illustrated by Ted Enik and would appreciate any information that would enable us to do so.

Illustrators, other than those acknowledged in each story, include Jean Cooper Brown pp.54-57; Wendy Elks p.48; Ted Enik p.63; Ian Forss pp.17,18-26 (colouring), 27; Peter Foster pp.6-16; Jack Hanna pp.4-5; Laurence Hutchins pp.28-49; Geo Parkin p.64; Chris Ryley pp.50-53; Chris Winn pp.60-61.

We would like to thank The Metropolitan Police and the Essex Police Dog Training Section for their help and advice on the article, 'Fascinating facts about police dogs'.

CONTENTS

GET THE GOLD TO

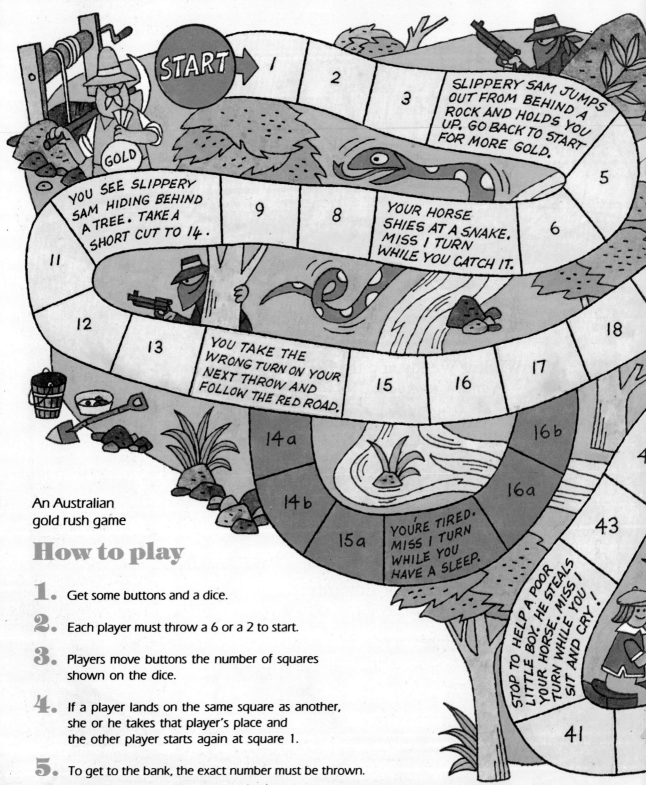

START

GOLD

1 2 3

SLIPPERY SAM JUMPS OUT FROM BEHIND A ROCK AND HOLDS YOU UP. GO BACK TO START FOR MORE GOLD.

5

YOU SEE SLIPPERY SAM HIDING BEHIND A TREE. TAKE A SHORT CUT TO 14.

9 8

YOUR HORSE SHIES AT A SNAKE. MISS I TURN WHILE YOU CATCH IT.

6

11

12 13

YOU TAKE THE WRONG TURN ON YOUR NEXT THROW AND FOLLOW THE RED ROAD.

15 16 17

18

14a

16b

14b

15a

16a

YOU'RE TIRED. MISS I TURN WHILE YOU HAVE A SLEEP.

43

STOP TO HELP A POOR LITTLE BOY. HE STEALS YOUR HORSE. MISS I TURN WHILE YOU SIT AND CRY !

41

An Australian gold rush game

How to play

1. Get some buttons and a dice.

2. Each player must throw a 6 or a 2 to start.

3. Players move buttons the number of squares shown on the dice.

4. If a player lands on the same square as another, she or he takes that player's place and the other player starts again at square 1.

5. To get to the bank, the exact number must be thrown.

Wildcat Wendy
and the
Peekaboo Kid

Wildcat Wendy and her friend the Peekaboo Kid were surrounded. What would they do if Headlock Henry found out where the treasure was hidden? Suddenly they heard a nasty voice from outside.

"Hey, you in there. Come out and show yourself."

The two friends in the hideout didn't move a muscle.

"You don't have to be afraid of me, little Miss Wendy," the voice said. "Come on out. You don't want me to take away your little horsey, do you?"

6

Wendy signalled to Peekaboo that she would go out by herself. Headlock Henry obviously hadn't seen Peekaboo, and thought Wendy was on her own.

She crawled out of the hide-out and stood up straight, facing Headlock Henry without a flicker. He had a gang of three with him, and they had her surrounded.

"I'm not little Miss Wendy—to you or anyone else," she said. "The name's Wildcat."

"I see," said Headlock Henry with a sneer on his face. "Well, little Miss Wendy, just you step aside and let us through. We know the treasure is in there, and we aim to get it."

Wendy hoped she had given Peekaboo time to plan an unpleasant surprise for Headlock. She tried to stall him a bit longer.

"The treasure isn't in there," she said. "It's in my saddle-bag. I'll show it to you."

Headlock Henry snorted. "Don't try to kid me," he said. "I've already searched your saddle-bag. Nothing precious in there. Get out of my way, missy."

Headlock shoved Wendy aside and entered the hide-out. His gang were preparing to follow him, and they weren't watching Wendy. Very cautiously, stealthy as a cat, she began to edge nearer to Victor.

When she was close enough, she swung up into the saddle, pulled her special long-handled fork from the saddle-bag, and charged straight at Headlock Henry's gang.

"Take that," she yelled, poking at one of them with her weapon. "And that," as she clipped another on the shoulder.

Victor was dodging and wheeling in order to keep Wendy out of the gang's clutches. He was a brave horse and didn't care if they hit him, so long as they couldn't reach Wendy.

The battle got wilder and wilder. As they fought, Wendy noticed that they were moving nearer and nearer to the stream.

"Hi-yi, Victor," she shouted. "Let's give 'em the bath of their lives."

Victor understood exactly what Wendy meant. He reared up and gave a mighty horse-scream. The gang stood petrified, not knowing what was happening.

Victor dashed at them at full tilt and, one by one, he toppled them right into the water.

"That's far more fun than bowling," Wendy said. "You *are* a clever horse."

Victor was breathing hard and feeling rather tired, but he gave a happy nod and a whuffle in reply.

They watched the gang spluttering and clambering out of the stream on the other side. The gang didn't even look back. They ran off into the forest as fast as their legs could carry them.

Wendy dismounted and walked back to the hide-out. She knelt down by the opening and strained her ears to hear what was going on inside.

"I can't hear a thing," she said finally. "You don't suppose they've knocked each other out, do you?"

Victor shook his head and went back to his grazing.

"Stone the crows," Wendy said to herself. "I can't sit here like a wet noodle. Better go inside and see whether it's good news or bad news."

The sight that met her eyes made her roar with laughter. She laughed and laughed until the tears came.

"Why," she gasped, "why, if it isn't little Miss Henry!"

Wendy exploded into whoops of laughter again, because there was Henry — big, tough Headlock Henry — neatly rolled up in the brown blanket and tied with rope all round. But what really tickled Wendy most was the sight of Headlock's head.

For there, stuck firmly between his open jaws, was one of the juicy green apples.

"It was the only way to keep him quiet while I went out to make sure the rest of the gang had vamoosed," the Peekaboo Kid said later to Wendy.

They were sitting by a blazing campfire, sharing the other apple, the cheesy biscuits, and some clear cold stream water out of the mug.

"Well, I'm glad H.H. promised not to yowl any more," Wendy said. "I know he's a bully, but I'd hate to leave him with an apple stuck in his mouth all the way back to town."

Peekaboo nodded.

"Are we going to stay here tonight?" Wendy asked. "I'd better get Victor settled, if we are."

"I reckon we should get back to town kind of quickish," Peekaboo said. "Tiny John will be worried about us. We can set off as soon as the full moon rises. I'll be able to see well enough then."

"O.K.," Wendy said. "We don't dare untie little Miss Henry, so we'd better strap him on Victor's back for the journey. Right? And I'll walk with you."

"Wildcat," said Peekaboo, "why do you call him little Miss Henry?"

Wendy scowled and said, "No one calls *me* little Miss Wendy more than once and gets away with it."

"I see," said Peekaboo, and changed the subject. "Let's have a marshmallow."

Wendy stuck a marshmallow on the prongs of her long-handled fork and held it over the fire. When the marshmallow was nicely burnt on the outside and sweet and runny on the inside, she gave it to Peekaboo.

"Yum," he said. "That was delicious."

"And very nourishing," said Wendy.
"And there are twenty-three more marshmallows still to eat."

"That's just dandy," said the Peekaboo Kid, and he settled down to wait for the rise of the full moon.

Story by Nancy Chambers, illustrated by Peter Foster.

SHERLUCK BONES AT THE BISCUIT FACTORY

Sherluck Bones, the world-famous detective, lives in Kennelwood, U.S.A. His good friend Scotson lives there, too. Together they have solved many mysteries, crimes, and puzzling events around town. No clue escapes the eagle eye of Bones. No puzzle is too hard for his quick brain to solve.

18

See if you're as good a detective as Bones is. At the end of this story (on p. 26) there is a question to be answered. There is a clue in the story to help you, so pay attention and try to come up with the solution along with Bones and Scotson.

The Kennelwood biscuit factory was famous for its chocolate chip biscuits. Everyone in Kennelwood loved them. The owner of the factory, Sally Spitz, was a good friend of Sherluck. One day Bones and Scotson decided to pay her a visit. Sally met them at the gate and took them for a tour of the factory. They walked past big vats full of hot melted chocolate.

There were mounds of biscuit dough on tables and many busy biscuit cutting machines. Scotson was getting hungry as he watched the biscuits being made. Then Sally took them to the bakery where the biscuits were baked. Bones was very interested in everything.

"I understand that the recipe for your chocolate chip biscuits is a secret," he said to Sally.

"Yes," she answered "We keep the recipe in a big safe that has a burglar alarm."

"I say," said Scotson, "I'm sure no thief would ever be able to steal *that* recipe."

"Yes," Sally answered, "and as a double protection, we have a night watchman. He is here from seven o'clock in the evening until nine o'clock in the morning.

"An alert fellow, I suppose?" asked Bones. Sally said that she thought so but didn't know for sure, since he was new. She went on to explain that her regular night watchman was on holiday. A fellow named Marvin Mastiff had been hired to take his place. Last night had been his first time on the job. Bones nodded.

Since it was about nine in the morning, they happened to meet Marvin coming from work. He was a big, slow-moving fellow. Sally stopped to talk to him.

"Well, Marvin," she said, "how did you get on with your first night on the job?"

F ine," he said. "I had no trouble at all."

Sally turned to Bones to say something, when Marvin interrupted.

"Say, I almost forgot," Marvin said. "Last night I had a dream that the burglar alarm was broken. My dreams usually come true." Marvin puffed out his chest and tried to look important. "So I suggest that you have the alarm checked."

Sally looked surprised and said that she would do that right away. Marvin just nodded and went off saying, "Well, I'd better go home and get some rest. I want to be alert again tonight."

24

Sally smiled and she turned to Bones. "Well, I'm impressed with Marvin," she said. "He certainly looks as if he knows what he's doing. I'm going to check that alarm right now."

"Before you do that," said Bones, "why don't you look for a new night watchman?"

Scotson and Sally opened their mouths in surprise.

Why do you say that?" sputtered Sally.

"Because Marvin is a very bad night watchman," answered Bones.

"But how can you know that, Bones?" asked Scotson. "You hardly know the fellow."

"I know enough to know that he should be fired," answered Bones. He then went on to explain why.

Do you know why Marvin was a bad night watchman?

Marvin said that he had a "dream" that the alarm was broken. If he was dreaming, he must have been asleep on the job. Bones realised that fact right away and told Sally.

by Jim and Mary Razz
illustrated by Ted Enik

Follow That Bus!

Miss Beaver and Class 6 are going on a visit to a farm. But on her way to school Miss Beaver leaves her bag on the bus. When she and the children go to get it, the bus is taken over by two bank robbers. They have a black holdall bag just like the teacher's, but their's is full of money that they've stolen. The robbers escape from the bus with the wrong bag. Miss Beaver and Class 6 arrive at the farm to meet Mr and Mrs Ramsbottom . . . . .

The children stared at the couple in amazement.

They could hardly believe their eyes.

The farmer was ugly enough, with his tiny, close-set eyes and his squashed nose, and the hideous scars that ran across his face from one cauliflower ear to the other.

But his wife! She was incredible!!! She was dressed in what looked like a long nightdress and wellingtons. The scarf she had wrapped round her huge head and tied under her enormous chin managed to conceal some of the face. But the bit that showed was astonishing.

Her face was so thick with powder she looked as if someone had tipped a bag of flour over her head and she'd forgotten to blow afterward. Her stubby eyelashes were white, her thick bushy eyebrows were white, and even the rims of her watery eyes were white. And somewhere near the bottom of the whiteness was a gash of brilliant red lipstick, which covered the whole of her mouth and most of her chin. She had a broken nose, and when she smiled coyly at them, her front two teeth were missing.

"Blimey!" whispered Avril, instinctively taking a step backward with the rest of the class.

"Hello," said Miss Beaver bravely, holding her hand out hesitantly to the farmer. "You must be –" she fumbled for the map again and looked at it – "Mr Ramsbottom."

"Yeah," said the farmer, nudging his wife, "Ramsbottom. That's our name."

"And you must be Mrs Ramsbottom," Miss Beaver added, offering her hand to the farmer's wife, as the farmer had ignored it.

The farmer's wife grunted and shuffled her feet.

"She don't say much," the farmer said, tapping his forehead and nudging his wife again. "On account of she's got a few screws loose."

"Oh!" said Miss Beaver, startled by the farmer's bluntness. "I'm Miss Beaver from New End School," she added nervously, "and this is Class 6."

"Wotcher!" the farmer said, glancing furtively at the children. His eyes rested on Avril, who was clutching the teacher's holdall tightly, mesmerised by the farmer's wife.

"'Ere," he said, taking a step toward her. "What's a little tiddler like you doing heaving a great heavy bag like that around for?"

He bent down and looked into Avril's eyes.

"I'll carry it for you," he said coaxingly.

Avril gripped the handle even tighter.

"You ain't got no bull," she said accusingly.

"What?" said the farmer, stepping back in surprise. Miss Beaver laughed uncertainly.

"I'm afraid Avril was rather disappointed that you didn't have a bull," she explained, "so I said she could carry my bag. It isn't heavy," she added. "It only has my handbag and raincoat in it."

"Well, I wouldn't want you to think I wasn't no gentleman, now, would I?" said the farmer, gritting his yellow teeth into a grin, and tugging at the bottom of the holdall.

Avril put both arms round the bag and pulled back, staring defiantly at the farmer, whose grin was fading rapidly.

"I expect she'll get tired of carrying it soon," Miss Beaver said hastily, not wanting to hurt the farmer's feelings.

The farmer muttered to himself and let go suddenly. "Yeah!" he said, scowling, as Avril fell backward. "She'd better – I mean I'd feel better," he added quickly, helping an indignant Avril to her feet, "carrying it myself."

He lowered his voice and clasped his hands together tightly. "You see, I just love children. And it breaks my heart to think of the poor little things going and straining themselves, like. You know what I mean?"

Miss Beaver nodded politely, although she didn't know what he meant at all.

The children had begun whispering amongst themselves, and Miss Beaver, not wanting the farmer and his wife to overhear them, said very loudly, "It was awfully kind of you to offer to show us round the farm, but I'm sure we can manage on our own, can't we, children?" She turned desperately to the children who were whispering even louder now, and she was sure she heard Jessica murmur "Frankenstein" in Akbar's ear.

"YOU MUST BE TERRIBLY BUSY!" she shouted at the farmer, trying to drown the children's conversation.

"No, we ain't," said the farmer. "We ain't got nothing to do but show you round, have we, Missus?" He dug his elbow into his wife, who didn't seem to hear him as she stared foolishly at the ground.

"HAVE WE, MISSUS?" he repeated, clipping his wife smartly round the ear.

"Hey. Watch it!" his wife replied in a gruff, reproachful voice.

"Just a little playful larking about," said the farmer, laughing as he raised his fist and thumped his wife violently between the shoulder blades.

"The poor old girl's got a touch of laryngitis, ain't yer?" he roared in her ear.

His wife nodded slowly, then lifting her muscular arm, sent the farmer flying with a return clout.

The farmer staggered to his feet and advanced menacingly toward his wife.

The children held their breath, waiting for the
blow to fall. But the farmer, instead of hitting her,
tweeked his wife playfully on the cheek.

"As I was saying," he said cheerfully to Miss
Beaver, who was beginning to look a bit alarmed,
"just a little playful larking about. Now," he
added, glancing slyly at the breathless children,
and nudging his wife yet again, "to show these
little darlings around."

Dominic prodded Morgan, who had edged his
way to the front of the class.

"Please, sir," said Morgan politely, "you
haven't seen two masked men around, have you?
There was a robbery and we chased them, but
they got away."

"Masked men?" the farmer repeated vaguely.
"We ain't seen no masked men, have we,
Missus?" He thrust his face close to his wife's.

His wife shook her head vigorously.

"We ain't seen nothing," she squeaked in a
falsetto voice.

Goodness, thought Miss Beaver, her laryngitis
has cleared up quickly.

"Oh!" said Morgan disappointed.

Dominic nudged Morgan again.

"Then please could we have a ride on your tractor?" he added quickly.

"Please, Miss, I'm starving to death," Jessica complained. "Can't we have our picnic first?"

"I don't want to ride on no tractor," Avril said. "I want to look around the farm."

"We want a ride on the tractor too, Miss," the rest of Class 6 chorused.

"Well," said the farmer, stroking his chin thoughtfully. "I think I can keep you all happy, you know what I mean? The missus here can show Avril round the farm" – he patted Avril gently on the cheek, and winked slowly at his wife – "while I give the rest of you kids a quick turn on the tractor before you has your nosh."

Avril looked at the wife doubtfully, but finally muttered, "All right." The rest of the class, led by Miss Beaver, followed the farmer across to the tractor and trailer.

As Avril, still clutching the holdall tightly, went
into the barn with the farmer's wife, she noticed,
with surprise, a faint stubble of whiskers
protruding through the thick white powder on
Mrs Ramsbottom's face.

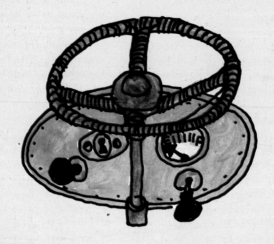

The children waited impatiently while the farmer,
glancing furtively over his shoulder toward the
barn all the time, fiddled with the knobs on the
tractor.

"I don't think he knows how to drive it,"
Morgan whispered to Dominic. The farmer
pressed every button and tapped every dial on the
dashboard, but still couldn't get the engine
started.

"Please, sir," said one of the littler children,
who was still not sure about the cows in the field.
"Are they cows or bulls over there?"

"Is what cows or bulls?" asked the farmer,
looking around vaguely.

"There!" said Jessica, stabbing her finger at the field. The farmer looked confused for a moment, then catching Dominic's eye, said, "You look like a smart lad, tell her what they are."

"Cows!" said Dominic proudly.

"Yeah!" said the farmer. "Cows. That's what they are."

"And what breed are the pigs?" Miss Beaver asked politely, as the farmer started kicking the tractor angrily, still peering anxiously in the direction of the barn.

"Pigs," said the farmer, "what pigs?"

"Why those," said Miss Beaver, glancing at the three sleepy pigs. The farmer looked at the pigs in desperation.

"Let's see," he said, stroking his chin. "Any smart kid know what breed these pigs is?"

Class 6 shook their heads.

The farmer looked relieved. "They're longhorns, ain't they?" he said.

"Please, sir," said Jessica, "I thought longhorns were cattle. I saw a film once, where a cowboy was trampled to death by longhorns . . ."

"Aha," interrupted the farmer, scowling at Jessica, "just trying to catch you out. You know what I mean?"

"They're shorthorns," he added fiercely, thrusting his face toward Jessica's.

Jessica stepped back nervously, then the farmer's scowl changed to an oily smile.

"Sharp as a razor blade, this 'un," he said to Miss Beaver, patting Jessica gently on her cheek.

The children were beginning to feel very hungry as they stood watching the farmer kicking the tractor and jerking his head toward the barn between each kick, and were quite relieved when Mr Coatsworth stuck his head out of the bus and shouted, "You forgot your lunch, Miss," and jumped down from the bus to join them, carrying Miss Beaver's sandwiches and his own packed lunch.

"Please, Miss," said Jessica, clutching her stomach. "I'm absolutely dying of starvation. I can't go another minute," she added dramatically, "without food."

"Neither can we, Miss," said the rest of the class, realizing that the chances of a ride on the tractor were getting very slim.

"Here!" Mr Coatsworth laughed and pulled a large bag of sweets from his pocket. "Have an aniseed ball to keep you going."

The children lost interest in the farmer when they saw the bag, and crowded round Mr Coatsworth as he handed out the sweets.

The farmer had lost interest in the children too, and was staring openly at the barn.

"I think," said Miss Beaver, "that if you don't mind we'd better have our picnic now." She glanced at her watch. "It's getting rather close to lunch time."

"Yeah!" muttered the farmer, shading his eyes and staring past her. "The old geezer don't seem to want to go anyway." His eyes suddenly lit up, as he caught a glimpse of his wife, lurking by the side of the house and beckoning furiously to him.

"I'm feeling a bit peckish myself," he said slowly. "I think I'll go and get some grub too."

What a strange gentleman, Miss Beaver
thought, as she and Mr Coatsworth followed the
children to the empty field.

"Here's a good spot, Miss," Akbar said,
spreading his raincoat on the damp grass and
sitting down.

Miss Beaver watched the rest of the children
spreading their raincoats out too, thinking she
would do the same, when she realized that hers was
in the bag that Avril was carrying. She looked
around, but couldn't see any sign of Avril.

"Has anyone seen Avril?"
she asked.
"She went off with the
farmer's wife," said Akbar,
"to look round the farm."
"That's funny," said
Morgan. "I saw the
farmer's wife go into
the house, but Avril
wasn't with her."

"Oh dear," said Miss Beaver. "I do hope she hasn't got lost. I think perhaps we ought to go and look for her," she added nervously.

"There she is!" Dominic shouted, as a dishevelled figure came tearing toward them, shouting at the top of its voice.

"Good heavens!" exclaimed Miss Beaver, grabbing Mr Coatsworth's arm. "Whatever is happening?"

For, not only was Avril shouting, but the bedroom window off the farmhouse had suddenly been thrown open, and two complete strangers, waving their arms wildly in the air, joined in the shouting too.

"Look!" yelled Morgan above the din.

Two figures, clutching black holdalls, were
running toward the bus.

"Oh no!" whispered Miss Beaver faintly, as one
of them nearly tripped over his long skirt and
threw the scarf (which had fallen over his eyes) to
the ground, revealing a shaven head.

"It's the robbers!" screamed the children,
jumping to their feet and chasing after Mr
Coatsworth, who was already racing after the
two crooks.

But they were too late. The bus engine started
up, and with Sid at the wheel and Bert clinging
tightly onto the door, the bus swerved out of the
farmyard and careered down the drive toward the
open road.

"Quick, kids! Into the trailer!" shouted Mr
Coatsworth, jumping into the driving seat of the
tractor. Avril and Miss Beaver caught up with the
rest of the class and threw themselves into the
trailer too.

The children were wild with excitement. They
bounced and swayed in the trailer, shouting and
screaming at Mr Coatsworth, urging him to go

faster as he desperately tried to catch up with the
retreating bus.

"He locked me in the barn," Avril kept yelling
indignantly. "When I said I thought he was really
a bloke, he grabbed the bag and locked me in the
barn."

"But what on earth did he want with my bag?"
Miss Beaver interrupted.

"And why were they pretending to be Mr and Mrs Ramsbottom?" asked Akbar.

"And how did they know we were going to the farm?" Dominic demanded.

"I still think they're spies," said Jessica wildly, "trying to get secret information about a deadly new substance that turns people invisible."

Dominic sighed. "I told you before," he said. "A raincoat, a handbag, and a roadmap aren't any use to a spy. Anyway," he added, "they're robbers, not spies."

Morgan, who had been listening to the conversation with a funny look on his face, jumped up suddenly.

"That's it!" he shouted.

The children stopped screaming at Mr Coatsworth and looked at him in astonishment.

"That's it!" he repeated, hanging onto the side of the trailer to steady himself. "The map!"

"See!" said Jessica proudly. "Morgan thinks they were after Miss Beaver's bag too!"

"But they didn't want Miss Beaver's bag!" Morgan cried. "Don't you see?" He turned to Miss Beaver. "Your holdall is exactly the same as the two they had. They must have got mixed up when they hijacked the 24 bus, and when they discovered the map in your bag, they knew we were going to the farm."

"So they disguised themselves as Mr and Mrs Ramsbottom," Dominic added slowly, "to try and get their holdall back!"

"Then that strange couple at the window must be the real farmer and his wife!" gasped Miss Beaver.

"And I," shrieked Avril, "have been walking round all morning with half their loot!"

Written by Pat Hutchins,
illustrated by Laurence Hutchins.

POLICE DOGS

Dogs have been used for "police" work throughout history. They have special qualities which make them suitable for this. These qualities are: a keen sense of smell, excellent hearing, and the ability to sense movement in the dark.

The earliest record of dogs being used for "police" work dates back to 1,000 BC in Egypt.

In the fifteenth century, dogs were taken on patrol by the parish constable.

In 1946, the first trained police dogs were used in London. These were Labradors.

The German Shepherd (Alsatian) is the most popular dog used for police work. This is because it has both highly developed senses and a high level of intelligence.

Labradors can also be used for patrol work, but are usually trained to do specialist work in searching for drugs and explosives.

Other breeds of dog used for specialist work

Springer Spaniel

Retriever

How is a police dog trained?

The police dog handler chooses a puppy when it is about three months old.

The puppy lives with the handler at his or her home. In this way, the puppy learns to trust and respect its handler.

For six months, the handler walks the puppy around the streets of the beat.

After one year, the dog begins his real training

Obedience

On the command of "heel", the dog learns to walk on the left side, close to the knee of the handler.

Tracking

The handler uses a tracking harness to teach the dog to use its sense of smell to follow a scent.

Criminal work

The dog learns to seize the right arm of the criminal, until the command of "leave" instructs it to let go.

What work does a police dog do?

Police dogs are useful in helping to search for missing people. Before setting out, the dog is given a piece of clothing to smell so that it learns the missing person's scent.

The speed and agility of the trained police dog is important in the chasing and cornering of criminals.

Specially trained "sniffer dogs" are used to help with the search for hidden drugs and explosives.

Diary of a Would-be Burglar

by Pat Edwards
illustrated by Jean Cooper Brown

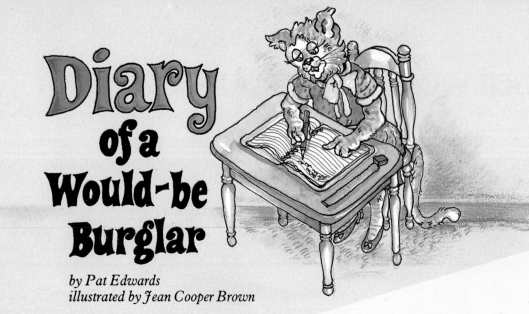

Monday   Dear Diary,

Dere   Last ~~nite~~ night I saw an exciting TV show.

It was about a ^cat burgl~~e~~r called Bill. He

has lots of adventures and makes lots

of ~~munny~~ money. I've decided to be a bur-

glar too.

Here's a list of what I need:

black ~~jenes~~ jeens pants

black jumper

black mask

torch

bag for all the things I'll ~~steel~~ steal.

That's all. It's time for ~~my fay~~ fae the

programme I like best now. It's called

Cops and robbers.

54

Tuesday
Dear Diary,
I ~~good~~ could only get an orange mask at the shop. I hope it will do. ~~Tonite~~ To-night I will rob my first house, but not till after ~~Detecktive~~ Detective Dan on TV.

Wens Wednesday
Dear Diary,
Last ~~nit~~ night I got all ~~reddy~~ ready to go out and be a burglar, but my

torch ~~wood~~ wouldn't work. I went next door to ask Mrs Plum if she had a spare ~~battry~~ battery, but she didn't. She was watching Burglar Bill too.

So I stayed and looked at it with her.
When I left she said she hoped I ~~enjoy~~
~~eyoid~~ had fun at my party. I ~~gess~~
~~guess~~ I ~~shood~~ shou^ld have taken my
mask off.

Friday
Dear Diary
Yesterday I got a new ~~batry~~ ~~battry~~ battery.
Then last ~~nite~~ night I went out to do ~~sum~~
some ~~burglaring~~ robbing as soon as
Policewoman Pauline was finished on TV.
The first house I went to I ~~shron~~ shone
my torch in the ~~windo~~ window to see what
they had had to ~~steel~~ steal, but the owner
came out and chased me all the way

56

around the block. Mr Sooty was putting his milk bottle out when we ran past. He said he was glad I had taken up jogging. I got home just in time to see the end of Slippery Sam the Trickster Man.

Saturday
Dear Diary,
I couldn't go out burgling last night because I wanted to watch the Catch-a-Crook programme. It was very disappointing. All the burglars got cort caught.

Monday
Dear Diary
I am not going to be a burglar after all. Last night I saw a new programme called The Cat from Mars, so now I'm going to be an astronort astronaught astronaut.
I wonder if I can buy a space ship in the supermarket?
Now it's time to watch Lost in Space, so that is all.

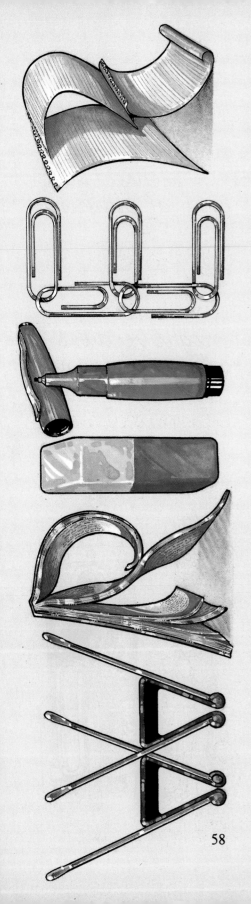

Meet

Name: *Pat Edwards*

Born at: *Invercargill, New Zealand, on 5 July 1925*

Started school at: *Bluff Public School New Zealand*

Favourite subject at school: *I had two. Art and Composition – which was what they called story-writing.*

What I didn't like about school: *Maths; teachers who yelled at us; sitting inside on a hot sunny afternoon.*

Favourite food when young: *a big slab of gingerbread and a cup of cocoa on a cold wet day; jelly and ice-cream on hot days.*

Favourite food now: *a bowl of chilli con carne and pecan pie.*

Best-loved story or book when young: *"Rin-tin-tin" (I loved dogs!)*

Pat Edwards

Favourite kind of books now: _science fiction and historical adventures._

Three things I love: _kids, cats, salted peanuts_

Three things I hate: _people being unkind to children, cats catching birds, olives_

Secret wish: _to learn to fly a small plane_

Favourite riddle: _What lies at the bottom of the ocean, trembling?_

A nervous wreck.

Pat Edwards invented us !

NOTHING, THAT'S WHAT

"What ARE you doing, Rupert?"
There comes the same reply,
For Rupert answers, "Nothing."
And that's his daily cry.

"What are you DOING, Rupert?
Who broke the garden pot?"
But Rupert answers, "Nothing."
And nothing's not a lot.

Whenever people blame him
For doing such-and-such
Then Rupert's doing nothing,
Which isn't very much.

"We want to SEE you, Rupert,
Who made his awful mess?"
But Rupert's doing nothing.
Well, nothing more or less.

And so we have this problem
To puzzle anyone,
How Rupert's doing nothing,
Yet naughty things get done.

Max Fatchen

Who's lying?

Claude left his new black biro on his desk when he went to the library. When he came back it was gone.

Have either of you taken my new biro?

George

Claude

Well, I didn't! I never left my desk.

And it wasn't me. Anyway I've already got a black one.

Bertha

Who's lying?

Claude knew Bertha Bandicoot was lying because he hadn't said what colour the missing biro was, yet Bertha mentioned that she already had a *black* one.

WANTED WORDS

Glossary

alert (*p. 22*)
wide-awake

Bandicoot (*p. 62*)
a large rat-type animal

bush (*p. 5*)
an Australian word for
wild, open country

bushranger (*p. 5*)
someone who takes to the
outdoors in Australia and
lives by robbery

cautiously (*p. 8*)
being very careful

clambering (*p. 11*)
climbing up on hands
and feet

clipped (*p. 9*)
hit him quickly

coyly (*p. 29*)
shyly

damper (*p. 5*)
a kind of bread cooked
on a campfire

dandy (*p. 16*)
lovely

Glossary continues on page 64

Not last night
but the night before
twenty-four robbers
came knocking at my door.
As I came out
to let them in
they stole some money
from the biscuit tin.

WANTED!

dishevelled *(p. 44)*
in a mess

falsetto voice *(p. 35)*
making your voice sound
higher than it usually is

gold rush *(p. 4)*
when many people rush
to a place where gold
has been found in order
to get rich quickly

laryngitis *(p. 34)*
an illness when you lose
your voice

mesmerised *(p. 30)*
fascinated

sneer *(p. 7)*
mocking look

trooper *(p. 5)*
an Australian mounted
policeman

vamoosed *(p. 12)*
went away

vats *(p. 19)*
huge tubs

whuffle *(p. 11)*
a noise a horse makes;
a very soft whinney;
a snuffle

yowl *(p. 14)*
a howl